The King's Pants

NICHOLAS ALLAN

ANDERSEN PRESS

D1494738

First published in Great Britain in 2023 by Andersen Press Ltd.,

20 Vauxhall Bridge Road, London, SW1V 2SA, UK

Vijverlaan 48, 3062 HL Rotterdam, Nederland

Copyright © Nicholas Allan 2023

Printed and bound in China.

British Library Cataloguing in Publication Data available.

ISBN 978 1 83913 362 6

1   3   5   7   9   10   8   6   4   2

The King likes to dress well . . .

. . . with many crowns

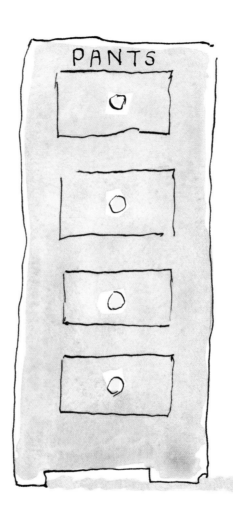

. . . and many pants.

Cedric is the Keeper of the King's Pants –
the Everyday Pants, the Weekend Pants . . .

and the Coronation Pants.
The King cannot be crowned without these.

(And the Pants Song *must* be sung.)

When the King goes away . . .

Cedric puts all the King's pants in a sack.

But one night the Royal Sack
got mixed up with a Royal Mail sack!

The next day there were *many* surprises in the post.

And the King had to have breakfast in his *kilt*!

Undercover police were sent to uncover the underwear.
Sniffer dogs were used to track them down!

And at last the pants were all found
(and thoroughly cleaned in the Royal Laundry).

That's when the King decreed that a great many more pants should be made for him, to stop any further accident.

Cedric checks them with the Royal Pants App.

H.R.H. ROYAL PANTS APP

MEETING THE PEOPLE

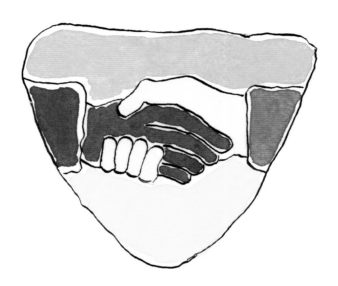

COUNTRY MATTERS

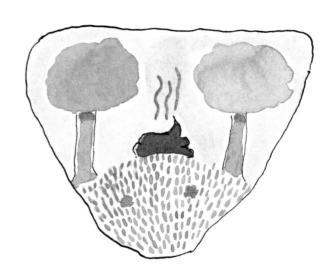

WAR PANTS

PEACE PANTS

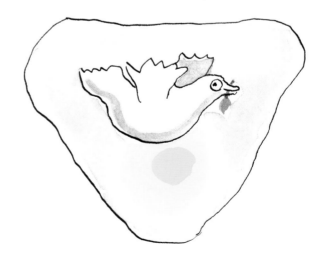

INTERNATIONAL

CASUAL ROYAL

VISITING THE MINT
(EXTRA POCKETS INCLUDED)

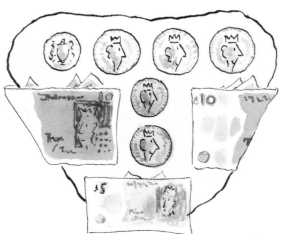

POSH ROYAL

(The app password is a state secret.)

The King even has Space Pants.
These are fitted with emergency air-bags.

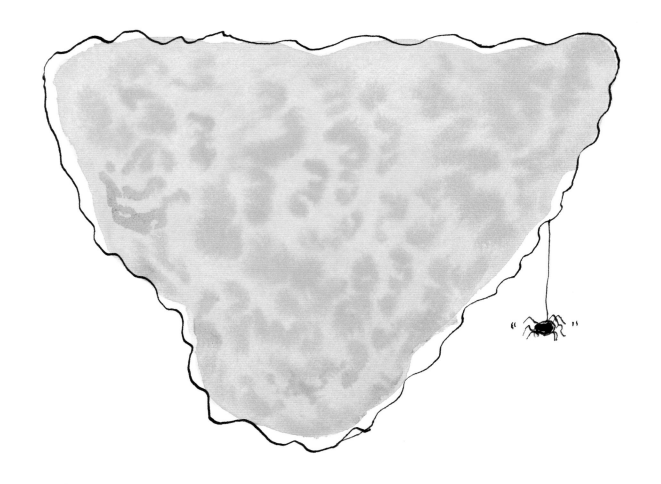

The Organic Pants are made with finest cotton,
wool from Welsh sheep and whole rolled oats
from the Scottish Highlands.

They are edible in emergencies.

And when the King goes to Windsor or Balmoral
he wears his Castle Boxer Shorts.

These are made by British cabinet makers
and have a working drawbridge . . .

. . . which can be very useful.

Soon the King found he had so many pants
he couldn't decide which to wear!

"Oh no! Not those! Oh no, not these! Oh no! Oh no!
No, no, *no*!"

So Cedric put all the pants in the sack
and asked the King to pull a pair out!

"Perfect!" said the King.

It did the King good to have a surprise.
Now he does this *every* morning.

So you never know which pants the King is wearing.

But if the King should decide to visit *your* school one day . . .

. . . you'll be able to ask him!